Penguin Study Notes

JOHN STEINBECK

Of Mice and Men

MARSAILI CAMERON, M.A.
Advisory Editor: STEPHEN COOTE, M.A., PH.D.

PENGUIN BOOKS

PENGUIN BOOKS

Published by the Penguin Group
Penguin Books Ltd, 27 Wrights Lane, London W8 5TZ, England
Penguin Putnam Inc., 375 Hudson Street, New York, New York 10014, USA
Penguin Books Australia Ltd, Ringwood, Victoria, Australia
Penguin Books Canada Ltd, 10 Alcorn Avenue, Toronto, Ontario, Canada M4V 3B2
Penguin Books (NZ) Ltd, Private Bag 102902, NSMC, Auckland, New Zealand

Penguin Books Ltd, Registered Offices: Harmondsworth, Middlesex, England

First published in Penguin Passnotes 1986
Published in Penguin Study Notes 1999
10 9 8 7 6 5 4 3 2 1

Interactive approach developed by Susan Quilliam

Set in 10/12.5 pt PostScript Monotype Ehrhardt
Typeset by Rowland Phototypesetting Ltd, Bury St Edmunds, Suffolk
Printed in England by Clays Ltd, St Ives plc

Contents

To the Student

The purpose of this book is to help you appreciate John Steinbeck's novel, *Of Mice and Men*. It will help you to understand details of the plot. It will also help you to think about the characters, about what the writer is trying to say and how he says it. These things are most important. After all, understanding and responding to plots, characters and ideas are what make books come alive for us.

You will find this book most useful after you have read the text you are studying through at least once. A first reading of the novel will reveal its plot and make you think about the lives of the people it describes and your feelings for them. Now your job will be to make those first impressions clear. You will need to read the novel again and ask yourself some questions. What does the writer really mean? What do I think about this incident or that one? How does the writer make such or such a character come alive?

This book has been designed to help you do this. It offers you background information. It also asks many questions. You may like to write answers to some of these. Others you can answer in your head. The questions are meant to make you think, feel and respond. As you answer them, you will gain a clearer knowledge of the novel and of your own ideas about it. When your thoughts are indeed clear, then you will be able to write confidently because you will have made yourself an alert and responsive reader.

Note: Double quotation marks are used in this book for words and phrases taken directly from John Steinbeck's work.

The page references are to the Penguin Twentieth-Century Classics edition.

Background to John Steinbeck

Born in the small town of Salinas, California, in 1902, John Steinbeck was the son of a schoolteacher and a mill manager. His grandparents on both sides of the family were immigrant settlers. The family was not well off, and the young John Steinbeck took a number of part-time jobs to earn money. He also spent as much time as he could exploring the California countryside in search of wildlife. This countryside provides the setting for many of his novels, including *Of Mice and Men*.

He started writing short stories while still at high school; but his academic career at Stanford University was a patchy one. He dropped out of college for two years and made a living from a variety of jobs, including field work on a ranch. This experience he put to good use when writing *Of Mice and Men* fifteen years later. Steinbeck returned to university but left without a degree. He had already started work, however, on *Cup of Gold*, a novel about Morgan the pirate which was to be his first published work.

In the next few years, Steinbeck found – and lost – several jobs, including those of reporter and caretaker. In 1930 he married Carol Henning, who helped to support him while he wrote. Publication of *Cup of Gold* in 1929 was followed by *The Pastures of Heaven* (1932), *To a God Unknown* (1933) and *Tortilla Flat* (1935); this last work became a best-seller and gave Steinbeck some financial independence.

In 1936 he started work on what was to become *Of Mice and Men*, a short novel set among migrant farm workers. This work was, he wrote in a letter, "a tricky little thing designed to teach me to write for the theatre". Originally entitled "Something That Happened", Steinbeck intended the novel to be "a study of the dreams and pleasures of everyone".

The book had an unfortunate start in life. "Minor tragedy stalked," wrote Steinbeck in a letter. "I don't know whether I told you. My setter pup, left alone one night, made confetti of about half my manuscript book. Two months of work to do over again. It sets me back. There was no other draft. I was pretty mad but the poor little fellow may have been acting critically. I didn't want to ruin a good dog for a manuscript I'm not sure is good at all. He only got an ordinary spanking with his punishment fly swatter. But there's the work to do over from the start."

When the book was published in 1937, it was re-titled *Of Mice and Men*. Taken from the poem 'To a Mouse', by the eighteenth-century Scottish poet, Robert Burns, the title carries echoes of this other writer who was deeply involved in the lives of men working on the land. The phrase is found in the following lines from Burns' poem:

> But, Mousie, thou art no thy lane
> In proving foresight may be vain:
> The best-laid schemes o' mice and men
> Gang aft a-gley,
> And lea'e us nought but grief and pain
> For promised joy.
>
> Still thou art blest, compared wi' me!
> The present only toucheth thee:
> But och! I backward cast my e'e
> On prospects drear!
> And forward, though I canna see
> I guess and fear.

The book was instantly successful in terms of sales; and Steinbeck soon began work on a stage version. His collaborator, George Kaufman, an eminent director and writer of the time, commented that, 'It drops almost naturally into play form and absolutely nobody knows that better than you.' The play proved a considerable success on Broadway in New York and won the esteemed Drama Critics' Circle Award. In 1939 a film of the book was released.

Familiar with migrant working conditions since his time at high school and Stanford, Steinbeck expressed his anger and compassion in articles for newspapers and magazines. These feelings are also to be found in passionate form in novels such as *In Dubious Battle* (1936) and in what many consider his greatest work, *The Grapes of Wrath* (1939).

Too old for military service when America entered the war, Steinbeck wrote a book on the US Air Force to help boost recruitment; he also spent six months at the front as a correspondent for the *New York Herald Tribune*.

Steinbeck's first marriage broke down in 1942, and in 1943 he married a dancer, Gwen Verdon. The couple settled in New York and had two sons, but this marriage also ended in divorce. In 1950 Steinbeck married Elaine Scott.

Steinbeck's later work included screenplays, travel writing and more novels, including *The Pearl* (1947) and *East of Eden* (1952), a story which became familiar to many through the film starring James Dean. Steinbeck travelled a good deal, both in America and in Europe. In the 1950s and 1960s he became more politically active, writing condemnations of the Communist-hunting Senator Joseph McCarthy and campaigning vigorously on behalf of Lyndon Johnson, who became President after the assassination of John F. Kennedy. The 1960s also brought many literary awards, including the Nobel prize in 1962.

John Steinbeck died in 1968, after a series of illnesses.

Summary

Scene 1: *pp. 1–16*

John Steinbeck introduces us first of all to a place: a clearing on a wooded riverbank where a path ends up at a deep, green pool (p. 1). In the evening of a hot day, two men appear in the clearing (p. 2). When Lennie drinks thirstily from the pool, George warns him sharply that the water may not be fresh. They sit by the pool (p. 4).

Complaining about Lennie's bad memory, George reminds him that an employment agency has sent them into the country to work (p. 5). Lennie has been playing with a dead mouse and George takes this away from him. George also tells him not to open his mouth in front of the boss at the ranch where they are to work (p. 6).

Lennie is sent to get wood for a fire (p. 8) but comes back holding only one small stick. Realizing that Lennie has gone in search of the mouse, George makes him give it up, and throws it far away (p. 9). George reminds Lennie how, when he had mice as pets, he used to kill them by accident (p. 9).

After Lennie has fetched more wood, George lights a fire and starts to heat some cans of beans. Lennie says that he likes beans with ketchup and George loses his temper (p. 11). He accuses Lennie of being a burden on him and always getting him into trouble, like when people thought Lennie had attacked a girl (p. 11). Lennie offers to go away, alone, to the hills; but George tells him that he wants him to stay.

Lennie then asks George to tell him "about the rabbits" (p. 13). Telling what is clearly a familiar story, George describes to Lennie how one day, unlike other ranch hands, the two of them will have a little place of their own (p. 14). While they have supper, George tells

Lennie to come back to the clearing if he gets into trouble again (p. 15). They lie down to sleep (p. 16).

Scene 2: *pp. 17–37*

It is ten in the morning (p. 17), and an old man is showing George and Lennie which bunks to take at the ranch's sleeping quarters. George complains that the bunk-house isn't clean but the old man denies it (p. 18). He also tells them that the boss is angry because they didn't turn up for work that morning (p. 18).

When the boss comes into the bunk-house, he complains to George and Lennie about their lateness; George offers an excuse for this (p. 21). The boss becomes suspicious of the fact that George is doing most of the talking (p. 22); and, after warning George not to be "a wise guy", the boss leaves (p. 23). While George is telling Lennie off for opening his mouth in front of the boss (p. 23), he discovers the old man outside the door. The old man denies the charge of eavesdropping.

A young man, Curley, comes into the room looking for the boss, his father (p. 25). Catching sight of Lennie, he becomes aggressive and tries to make him talk (p. 25). After Curley leaves, the old man tells George that Curley is an experienced boxer (p. 26); but George replies that Lennie could make short work of him (p. 26). According to the old man, Curley's recent marriage has made him even more aggressive. His wife, apparently, still has an eye for other men (p. 28). When the old man has gone, George tells Lennie to try to avoid Curley (p. 29); but, if he gets into any kind of trouble, to go back to the clearing by the river (p. 30).

Curley's wife appears in the bunk-house, saying that she's looking for Curley. Lennie thinks that she's pretty but George doesn't like the way she talks to them (p. 32). After she has gone, George gives Lennie a fierce warning to stay away from her.

Slim, the leader of one of the work teams, comes into the bunk-house and speaks in a friendly way to George and Lennie (p. 34). When another man, Carlson, joins them, it comes out in conversation that Slim's bitch has just had puppies (p. 35). Curley suggests that the old man, Candy, should shoot his dog and take one of Slim's puppies. When Carlson and Slim leave the room, Lennie and George discuss the possibility of Lennie's getting one of the puppies too (p. 36). Curley comes in looking for his wife and exchanges a few unfriendly words with George; George and Lennie then leave to find their dinner (p. 37).

Scene 3: *pp. 38–65*

It is evening in the bunk-house and George and Slim sit down to talk (p. 38). George thanks Slim for giving a puppy to Lennie; he is then drawn into talking about how he and Lennie have ended up travelling together (p. 39). He and Lennie, he says, have got used to each other (p. 40) – although Lennie does often get into trouble, like on the recent occasion when a girl mistakenly accused him of attacking her (p. 41). Lennie comes in and goes straight to his bunk, hiding the puppy that he is carrying. Undeceived, George sends him away to take the puppy back to its mother (p. 43).

When Candy and Carlson come in from playing horseshoes, Carlson starts complaining about the smell from Candy's old dog (p. 44). Carlson claims that it would be kinder to the dog to shoot it now rather than let it linger on. But Candy is reluctant to take this decision. Slim agrees with Carlson (p. 45).

The discussion is interrupted by the entrance of another ranch hand, Whit, who is anxious to show Slim a magazine (p. 46). Refusing to be distracted, Carlson presses Candy to agree to the shooting of the dog; he produces his Luger pistol in readiness. When Slim says nothing, Candy agrees, miserably (p. 47).

After Carlson has taken the dog, several attempts to engage Candy in conversation fail; George and Whit sit down together at the card table (p. 49). Eventually, the sound of a shot is heard (p. 49).

Crooks, the black ranch hand in charge of the stable, appears, and asks Slim to go with him to the barn. While playing cards, Whit and George talk about Curley's wife (p. 51). They agree that her presence seems likely to cause trouble on the ranch; Whit then asks George to join himself and the others the following night on a visit to the local brothel (p. 52). A few minutes after Carlson and Lennie return to the bunk-house, Curley bursts in, asking if anyone has seen his wife or Slim (p. 53). When he hears that Slim is in the barn, he dashes out, closely followed by Whit and Carlson (p. 54).

Lennie tells George that Slim has told him not to pet the pups so much; he also says that Curley's wife hasn't been in the barn. George expresses his worry about the set-up on the ranch (p. 56) and goes on to describe in detail the place which he and Lennie hope to get someday (p. 57). Lennie asks George to tell him exactly how he, Lennie, will care for the rabbits they will keep (p. 58). When Candy joins in the conversation, George is suspicious at first but listens quietly to Candy's proposal that he should contribute his savings and join in the scheme (p. 59). After doing some calculations, George realizes that their dream may now be within their grasp (p. 60). Greatly excited, the three decide to leave the ranch after a month; but George cautions them against telling anyone of their plans. Candy adds sadly that he should have shot his dog himself (p. 61).

Slim returns to the bunk-house, accompanied by Curley, Carlson and Whit. When Slim warns Curley to leave him alone, Curley looks around for someone to vent his rage on. He picks on Lennie (p. 62). Lennie is reluctant to fight back but, urged on by George, he seizes Curley's fist and crushes it; the fight is finished (p. 64). Before Curley is taken away to a doctor, Slim makes him promise not to tell anyone that it was Lennie who hurt his hand (p. 64). George reassures Lennie that he is not in trouble this time (p. 65).

Scene 4: *pp. 66–83*

Crooks, the "stable buck", has his living and sleeping quarters in the harness room (p. 66). Lennie comes to this room on Saturday night and, unsuccessfully at first, tries to make friends with Crooks (p. 68). After Lennie has explained that the others have gone into town and that he, Lennie, has been looking at the pups in the stable, Crooks softens a little and tells Lennie to sit down (p. 69).

In conversation, Lennie lets slip the secret of the planned-for land

(p. 69); Crooks reacts by mocking Lennie's friendship with George (p. 70). When Crooks mentions the possibility of George's not coming back, Lennie advances threateningly on him; but is slightly placated by Crooks's explanation that loneliness lies behind his mockery (p. 72). Crooks reminisces affectionately about his childhood on his father's ranch, but casts scorn on Lennie and George's dream of land of their own (p. 74).

Candy joins the two men in Crooks's room (p. 75) and the talk turns again to the dream of land. Fiercely, Candy defends their plans against Crooks's mockery (p. 76). Impressed despite himself, Crooks offers to come and help.

On the appearance of Curley's wife, the men fall silent and sullen – apart from Lennie who is fascinated (p. 77). When Curley's wife tries to find out what happened to Curley's hand, Candy tells her that he got it caught in a machine; a lie which she rejects angrily (p. 78). Stung by the insults which she has directed at them, Candy tells her that they have land of their own. Unconvinced, she notices the bruises on Lennie's face and works out that it was he who hurt Curley (p. 80).

Candy tells her to leave Lennie alone; and Crooks demands that she leave his room. Curley's wife turns viciously on Crooks, threatening him with terrible punishment (p. 81). Telling her that he has heard the men coming back, Candy urges her to go away; but, after she has gone, Crooks has lost all heart for the project (p. 82). George appears and scolds Lennie and Candy for talking about their plans (p. 83).

Scene 5: *pp. 84–98*

It is Sunday afternoon and all the ranch hands except Lennie are playing horseshoes outside. Lennie is sitting in the barn looking sorrowfully at the puppy, which he has just killed by accident (p. 85). Worried that George will punish him, he debates what to do until, suddenly, Curley's wife appears beside him and tries to draw him into conversation (p. 86).

Although Lennie attempts to avoid talking to her, Curley's wife wins him over by sympathizing about the puppy's death (p. 87). Going on to talk about her earlier life, she expresses resentment over lost hopes and opportunities (p. 89). The conversation turns to Lennie's dream farm and rabbits; Lennie explains that he likes rabbits because they are soft to touch (p. 90). Curley's wife then invites him to feel her hair but, when his hand is heavy on her head, she gets angry and screams (p. 91). In a panic, Lennie tries to silence her but, when she continues to scream, he shakes her angrily. This breaks her neck (p. 91).

Frightened at what he has done, Lennie remembers what George said about going back to the clearing and he leaves the barn (p. 92). Curley's wife lies undisturbed, peaceful in death, until Candy comes into the barn; on discovering the dead body, he leaves again, quickly (p. 93).

Candy returns to the barn with George, who immediately realizes how Curley's wife has met her death; the two men discuss what is to be done (p. 94). George decides that the other men must be told what has happened; but he asks Candy to give him a few minutes' start before the news is broken (p. 95). After expressing his rage and disappointment over his lost dreams, Candy fetches the other men. Curley immediately identifies Lennie as the killer and goes off to get his shotgun (p. 96). He returns to the barn with Carlson, who says that his Luger has been stolen; assuming that Lennie has taken it, Curley expresses his intention of shooting Lennie on sight (p. 96). George is forced to join the hunting party; while Candy is told to stay with the dead woman (p. 98).

Scene 6: *pp. 99–107*

It is late afternoon in the clearing by the river and Lennie comes out of the brushwood to drink from the pool (p. 100). Sitting by the river, he wonders to himself how George will treat him now; in his imagination his Aunt Clara scolds him for being a burden on George (p. 101). An imaginary giant rabbit then appears to him (p. 101) and threatens that this time George will leave him.

When George himself comes to the pool, he calms Lennie down and they sit silently while the shouts of the searching men come from a distance (p. 103). Puzzled that George doesn't seem angry with him,

Lennie encourages him to tell the familiar stories about the two of them, together and alone (p. 104). George asks Lennie to turn his head and look across the river while he, George, tells him how things will be; meanwhile, unseen, George takes Carlson's Luger out of his pocket (p. 105).

The distant voices come nearer and, after reassuring Lennie that he isn't angry with him, George shoots him in the back of the head (p. 106). The other men from the ranch burst into the clearing; George pretends that he has taken Carlson's gun away from Lennie in a struggle. Understanding something of what George is going through, Slim leads him gently away (p. 107).

Commentary

Scene 1: *pp. 1–16*

Do you know where Soledad is? Or the Salinas river? Judging by the first sentence of *Of Mice and Men*, John Steinbeck seems to think that you, the reader, probably do know where these places are. In fact, they are in California, in the United States of America, some way south of San Francisco.

Perhaps you feel that it doesn't matter where the story is set? Well, you'll find as you study the book that John Steinbeck is a writer who is very keen to help you really join him in his story. He wants you to hear, see, smell – and sometimes taste and touch – the life that he's introducing you to.

Take another look at the scene described on pp. 1 and 2 before the arrival of George and Lennie. There is a lot of life there by the pool, although most of it isn't human life; jot down some of the sights and sounds found there.

When George and Lennie appear, walking towards the pool, you'll see that John Steinbeck introduces them very carefully. Even before they speak a word, we know quite a lot about them. Look at the following pieces of information given to us and note down what they tell us about the two men.

1. Both wear denim clothing.
2. Both carry blanket rolls.
3. One man lags behind the other, even in the open clearing.
4. One man is neat, quick and restless.
5. The other man is big and cumbersome, moving like a bear.

By the time you've done this, you'll probably have realized just how much you already know or can guess. The two men are the same in some ways, aren't they, and different in others? Have you noted, for example, that the kind of clothes they're wearing probably show that they are working men – and that the blanket rolls they both carry indicate that they are used to being on the move? As for the differences between the men – well, it's quite clear already, isn't it, that one is the leader and the other the follower?

This initial impression is deepened once the men start exchanging words with each other. Would you think it was fair to say that George treats Lennie rather like a child? What words and actions of George's would prompt you to say this? And does Lennie in fact speak and behave like a child? In what ways does he do this?

After they've both drunk some water and sat down by the pool, George starts complaining about having been forced to walk so far in the heat. When Lennie shows that he has forgotten where they're going, George snaps at him and calls him "a crazy bastard". Look again at this section and at the following conversation on p. 5. Do you think that George is really angry with Lennie at this point? What evidence would you give to back up your opinion?

You may well have decided that George isn't really angry with Lennie; that he uses terms like "crazy bastard" in an affectionate rather than insulting way. Do you ever pretend to be angry or grumpy when you don't really feel that way at all? Or do other people ever pretend to be angry with you? In what sort of relationship would either of these things happen?

If you agree that George isn't really angry here, what does this tell us about George's relationship with Lennie? Jot down your thoughts on this, adding them to the conclusions you came to earlier about whether George treated Lennie like a child. As we read on, you'll find that you'll need to think a good deal about the relationship between the two men. Keep notes on your thoughts as you go along.

When reading the conversation on p. 5, you may have got the feeling that you were eavesdropping; that is, listening in on a conversation not primarily meant for your ears. There's the mysterious mention of "the rabbits", for example, and the unexplained reference to "Murray and Ready's". You'll probably get this feeling again several times as you read on: John Steinbeck has written his book almost like a play, so that much of the information we need comes to us through conversation among the characters. What we must do as readers is listen carefully, remember as much as we can, even if we don't understand it immediately ("the rabbits", for example) and, when we're given enough hints, guess (like, for example, guessing from what else George says that Murray and Ready's is an employment agency).

The episode when George discovers that Lennie has a dead mouse and takes it from him tells us a great deal more about the two men. George clearly knows Lennie very well indeed; and Lennie clearly has some rather odd tastes – like petting dead mice. What else does this episode tell us about George and Lennie?

On pp. 6–7 George gives Lennie instructions on how he is to behave at the ranch where they are to work. We learn at least two things from this: one, how bad Lennie's mental concentration is and, two, the fact that Lennie got into trouble at the last place where they worked. Do you think that George is patient or impatient with Lennie at this point? Why do you think this?

George has decided that he and Lennie should spend the night in the clearing. Read again, on pp. 8–9, the description of how Lennie retrieves his mouse and is then found out by George. Imagine that you're Lennie and write down a brief note on how you felt during this episode. Then imagine you're George and briefly describe the different emotions you felt.

Look again at the part of the conversation (on p. 9) where George and Lennie discuss what happened to the live mice Lennie used to keep as pets. How does this point forward to the climax of the book?

Together, George and Lennie prepare and light a fire so that they can heat up their supper. Have you ever built – or helped to build – a campfire or bonfire? Does the passage on p. 10 remind you of that experience? In what ways was your bonfire different?

George loses his temper when Lennie says, for the second time, that he likes beans with ketchup. Is George really angry this time? What makes you think this? Even if you do decide that he is really angry, do you think that he means everything he is saying? When you lose your temper, do you sometimes say things you don't really mean? Try to remember the different things George says to Lennie: we'll come across them again much later in the book.

Lennie is frightened by George's outburst; but the two men make friends again quite quickly afterwards. Note that George does not apologize. How then do they manage to smooth over the harsh words? This time, try to remember what Lennie says to George: again, we'll come across his words much later in the book.

At last (p. 14), we learn what Lennie has meant by talking about "the rabbits". He and George have a story they tell each other (although George does most of the talking). The story is about how loneliness and despair can be driven away by friendship. George and Lennie reassure each other that, unlike other ranch hands, they have a future ahead of them. Protected and encouraged by each other, they will someday get a little place of their own where they will grow crops and keep animals (including rabbits). (Did you recognize the phrase "Live off the fatta the lan'" on p. 14? Try it with an American accent . . . Written 'properly', it would read "Live off the fat of the land" – a phrase which comes from the Bible and means 'live well and have the best of everything'.) Do you feel sympathetic towards George and Lennie's dream? Why do you think they have this dream? Do you think either of them believes that it will become reality some day? Do you ever have dreams of this kind? How would your dream be different from the one described here?

While they have supper, George tells Lennie to come back to the clearing if he gets into any kind of trouble. He also warns him that if he does get into trouble, he won't be allowed to tend the rabbits. Do you feel that the author is preparing you, the reader, for future happenings? How do you feel about the thought of Lennie getting into trouble?

Scene 2: *pp. 17–37*

We're told quite a lot about the inside of the bunk-house, the big room where the ranch hands sleep. When they're not sleeping, how do the men spend their time there? Would you like living in a bunk-house, do you think? What would you like or dislike about it?

The old man cleaning out the bunk-house is anxious to reassure George that the place is clean. Notice what he says about the previous occupant of George's bunk: that he "used to wash his hands even *after* he ate"? Did you find that a funny remark? As well as being quite amusing, this episode tells us about the fairly rough conditions that the ranch hands have to live in. What does it also tell us about the kind of man George is?

The boss is angry, the old man says, because George and Lennie didn't arrive in time to go out to work that morning; and as usual, the boss took his anger out on the "stable buck". (He's the hand who stays at the ranch and looks after the livestock and tackle.) The old man explains this by saying that the stable buck is a "nigger". Remember that this story was first published in America in 1937. How do you think most white people regarded black people at this time? Read again the section of dialogue from the bottom of page 19. The boss clearly feels that the colour of the stable buck's skin provides a good enough reason for treating him badly; but do you think that the old man and the other ranch hands share his attitude?

When he does appear, the boss doesn't waste many words, immediately asking George and Lennie to account for themselves. Do you get the impression that George is used to dealing with awkward questions from bosses? What might give you this impression?

Look at the middle of p. 21, at the sentence beginning, "George scowled meaningfully at Lennie . . ." What is it that Lennie has understood? If you're not sure, look back to the middle of p. 11.

The boss is suspicious of the fact that George is doing most of the talking, answering for Lennie as well as for himself. Why is the boss suspicious? What does he think Lennie is up to? What might this tell us about the boss himself? George tells the boss that Lennie is his cousin; do you think he is telling the truth here? What might suggest that he's making this up?

After the boss has gone, George turns sharply on Lennie. He is angry because he's afraid. What is George afraid of? Do you ever get angry with other people when, really, you're afraid for yourself or for them?

George thinks that the old man has been listening in on their conversation. Do you think that George is right in this – or do you believe what the old man says? (A "swamper" is an odd job man.) Why is it that George doesn't "like nobody to get nosey"? And what does the old man mean when he says "a guy on a ranch don't never listen nor he don't ast no questions" (p. 24)? Do you agree with the old man that the boss is "a nice fella"? And what do you think he means by "you got to take him right"? Jot down three words which you might use to describe the boss.

The conversation between Curley and George is even more difficult and uneasy than the previous conversation with his father, the boss. Look back to that earlier conversation (pp. 21–3) and then make a note of the similarities and differences between the two conversations.

Now look back at the notes you've made. Have you included as a similarity the point that both Curley and his father are in a position of power over George and Lennie? And have you noted as a difference the fact that Curley seems to be on the brink of threatening physical violence?

Notice, towards the top of p. 26, what George says about Curley: "Say, what the hell's he got on his shoulder?" Did you catch the reference? George is referring to the phrase 'a chip on his shoulder', meaning something like 'a grudge against the world'. George is wanting to know what's wrong with Curley, that he's so needlessly aggressive.

The old man is happy to talk about Curley. As we saw earlier, much of the information we need as readers is given to us through conversation between the characters. Read again the section from the top third of p. 26 (sentence beginning, "The old man looked . . .") to two-thirds of the way down p. 28 (sentence ending, "There's plenty done that . . ."). The following pieces of information are contained there; put them in the order in which we learn them.

1. The old man is frightened of Curley.
2. Curley has become even more aggressive since his recent marriage.
3. Lennie doesn't like fighting.
4. Curley's wife is pretty and hasn't let marriage dampen her interest in other men.
5. Curley is a good and experienced boxer.
6. Whatever he does, Curley won't get sacked, being the boss's son.
7. George has no doubt that if Curley and Lennie start fighting, Lennie will win.
8. Lennie doesn't know any boxing rules.
9. Curley is a small man who hates bigger men.

You'll probably have noticed that, although we've only met one of the new characters involved (Curley), we now have a pretty clear picture of how things are at the ranch – and how they might develop.

Once George and Lennie are left alone, George warns Lennie about the possible dangers ahead. How does Lennie react to George's warning? Do you think that George is giving Lennie the right advice? Why do you think this? Have you worked out what "get the can" and "plug himself up for a fighter" (both on p. 29) probably mean? The first means 'get the sack' and the second means 'get well known as a fighter'.

As the conversation develops between the two men, we see again how dependent Lennie is on George. Note down two examples of this from p. 30. What is your first impression of Curley's wife? Do you think that this is the impression that the author wanted to get across? What makes you think this? Now re-read pp. 31 and 32 and think about how she appears to Lennie and to George. Jot down some notes on the differences in their reaction to her; then use these notes to write a paragraph describing the differences.

After she has gone away, Lennie suddenly expresses the wish to leave the ranch at once; but George tells him they must stay. Do you feel that George is making the right decision at this point?

Read through the description of Slim on pp. 33–4. Jot down five words that tell you what Slim is like. Some phrases may have puzzled you in the description. A "jerkline skinner" is a mule driver who controls several animals with one rein. A "bull whip" is a long, plaited rawhide whip with a knotted end. A "wheeler" is the wheel horse – that is, the horse that follows the leader and is harnessed next to the front wheels. "Butt" you probably know: it means the hindquarters. And what about the point about his hands being like those of a temple dancer? Well, in traditional dancing in certain countries in Asia the hands are the focus of attention, being used with great skill and grace.

Slim's friendly first words to Lennie and George may also contain some unfamiliar words and phrases. "It's brighter'n a bitch outside", for example, means that the sun's light is very strong; and "punks" don't here go in for safety pins or spikey hair; they're just inexperienced young men.

After Carlson joins in the conversation, we learn two things that are to become important: one is that Slim's bitch has just had puppies; the second is that Carlson wants the old man, Candy, to shoot his old dog. Did you guess, like George did, that Lennie was bound to want one of the puppies?

Curley makes another brief and angry entrance – to be greeted very coldly by George. Do you think George should have behaved any differently at this point?

Scene 3: *pp. 38–65*

Their day's work over, George and Slim are talking in the bunk-house. Lennie has been given one of Slim's puppies, it seems; and he has also proved his strength during the afternoon's work.

Like the boss earlier in the day (p. 22), Slim comments on the fact that George and Lennie are so friendly. (You may have noticed, on p. 34, that Slim had already mentioned this.) How do you think Slim's attitude to their friendship differs from that of the boss? Notice how what Slim has to say about the life of most ranch hands echoes what George said much earlier to Lennie (pp. 13–14).

It is during this conversation between George and Slim that we find out how George and Lennie first got friendly with one another. (Can you remember the lie about this that George told the boss? If not, look back at p. 22.) George says that at first he used to play tricks on Lennie. What made him stop doing this?

Slim comments that a "guy don't need no sense to be a nice fella . . . Take a real smart guy and he ain't hardly ever a nice fella". Is this true, do you think? Can you think of people you know who would fit these descriptions?

During this same conversation, we also find out exactly what kind of trouble Lennie got into at the place where they used to work. This is a list of some of the things that happened; put them in the correct order.

1. George and Lennie hide in an irrigation ditch.
2. George hits Lennie over the head with a fence post.
3. Girl screams more loudly.
4. Lennie reaches out to feel the dress.
5. George and Lennie leave the area at night.
6. Lennie sees a girl in a red dress.
7. A lynch party is organized to go after Lennie.
8. Lennie gets confused and holds on tight to the dress.
9. George hears the screams and comes running.
10. Girl lets out a scream.
11. Girl tells the police that she has been raped.

Imagine that you're the girl in the red dress, and write down what you felt happened when Lennie touched your dress. Then imagine that you're Lennie, and describe these same few minutes after you touched the girl's dress. Which set of feelings do you find it easier to describe? Why?

By this time in the story, you should have a pretty good idea of what Lennie and George are like as people. Write down some words that you think describe them and then write a paragraph about each of them (you'll probably find it helpful to use the notes on their relationship that you started keeping when looking at Scene 1).

Lennie comes into the bunk-house, hiding the puppy under his jacket. You'll probably agree with Slim (p. 43) that this time George does treat him just like a child. Jot down notes on how exactly he does this.

After Candy and Carlson come into the bunk-house, the conversation turns again to what should be done about Candy's old dog. Why is the old man reluctant to shoot his dog? Do you think that you would feel the same in his position? If you've read the whole book already, you'll realize that this exchange between Candy and Carlson sheds some light on future events in the lives of Lennie and George. Make notes on how it does this.

Why do you think the author introduces an interruption here in the shape of Whit's excitement over the magazine? Would you agree that at least two purposes are served by it? One is that the episode shows us that Carlson is determined not to be diverted from his goal of having the dog put down. The other is that we learn something more about what kind of people the ranch hands are and what kind of dreams and ambitions they have. Remember what we've already been told about Western magazines on p. 17? Jot down some thoughts on what kind of people you think they are (do they find their own lives exciting and fulfilling, for example?).

As we have seen, Slim's opinion is law in the bunk-house; and Slim has indicated that Carlson is right to shoot the dog. Candy can do nothing more to save him. Imagine that you're Candy after the dog has been taken away. Remembering all the things that we've been told about Candy and the dog (like, for example, that he's had him from the time he was a puppy), write an account of the main feelings that sweep over you as Candy.

While Candy lies silent on his bunk, the other men try to start up a normal conversation. You'll probably agree that they're not very successful in doing this. Why does their attempt not work?

After the shot has been heard, the atmosphere in the bunk-house becomes a bit more relaxed. While George and Whit play cards, Slim follows Crooks out to the barn. What news has Crooks brought about Lennie? From everything you've heard so far, how would you describe Lennie's approach to the puppies?

When Whit goes on to talk about Curley's wife, he echoes much of what Candy told George earlier. How would you summarize this?

George too echoes his own earlier words when he says, "She's gonna make a mess." Do you agree that by this time we, as readers, have a strong feeling that trouble of some kind is brewing?

Like all the ranch hands, Whit uses a lot of slang, some of which may be unfamiliar to you. Let's look more closely at the passage where he describes to George "the usual thing" done by the ranch hands on Saturday nights (p. 52). The "place" he's talking about is a brothel. If you don't know the meaning of that word, look it up in a dictionary. What word would you use? When George asks him how much it costs, he answers "two an' a half", meaning two and a half dollars. By a "short" he means a drink, a measure of spirits (probably whisky); and by "two bits" he means a quarter (25 cents). "A flop" refers to a sexual encounter with one of the women in the brothel.

Whit goes on to tell George that there are two rival brothels in town: Susy's place and Clara's. Susy's place is more fun, says Whit, and it's cheaper too. Susy thinks that Clara is stuck-up for no good reason (a "kewpie doll lamp" means a lamp that looks like a certain kind of doll – small, fat-cheeked and wide-eyed, with a curl of hair on top of the head). Indeed, Susy is in the habit of hinting to her customers not only that Clara overcharges (that's the meaning of "getting burned" at the bottom of p. 52) but that the women there may pass on some nasty diseases (that's the meaning of the following sentence, beginning "There's guys around here . . ."). "A crack" has the same meaning as "a flop"; and "goo-goos" means foreigners of one kind or another.

Lennie and Carlson come into the bunk-house. While Carlson is cleaning his Luger pistol (remember that he has this gun – it becomes important later), he tells the others that Curley, as usual, is looking for his wife. When Curley himself comes in on this quest, he also asks for Slim and, on hearing that he is in the barn, leaves in angry haste. What does Curley suspect? Whit and Carlson follow him to see what happens. What do they hope to see?

Meanwhile George finds out from Lennie that although Slim is in the barn (he has told Lennie not to pet the pups too much), Curley's wife has not been there. How would you describe George's attitude to this whole situation? George then goes on to give his opinion that on the whole the safest place for women is in a brothel; outside it, if they're young and attractive (he uses the words "jail bait" and "tart" (p. 56), they usually cause trouble for men.

If you're a girl, you may be feeling a little besieged, attacked or left out by this point in the story. After all, nearly all the likeable or admirable characters so far have been men; the women in the story may seem to you either not very important or not very nice. Take a minute, if you're a girl, to note down your feelings about this aspect of the story; if you're a boy, make notes on what you imagine you might feel if you were a girl.

Lennie is more interested in rabbits than in women. When he asks George about the place they hope to buy some day, old Candy turns over on his bunk to listen. Why do you think that this conversation might attract his interest when the earlier ones didn't? Remember the earlier notes you made on the dreams of the ranch hands.

Re-read the section from p. 56 to the bottom of p. 58 where George describes their dream ranch. First, make notes on where and how they hope to live; then write two paragraphs describing their life there. Would you like to live like that? What would you like about it?

When Candy first speaks, Lennie and George are startled and seem to feel guilty. George also becomes suspicious. Why might they react in this way? Candy then goes on to offer his savings (why does he have so much saved?) as contribution to the project if only George and Lennie will let him join them in this scheme. Re-read pp. 59–60, then make notes on why Candy is so anxious to join in (". . . they'll put me on the county" is the equivalent of "I'll have nowhere to live and only Income Support to live on").

How do George and Lennie react when they realize that their dream could become a reality? Do they react differently? If so, how? George is anxious that no one else should know about their plans. (Did you get the meaning of the sentence on p. 61 beginning, "They li'ble to can us . . ."? It means, "They're likely to get us sacked so that we can't save up the money we need.") Why do you think George might feel this way?

Notice what Candy says to George about feeling that he should have shot his dog himself. Why do you think he feels this? Think of the end of the story if you've read that far; why is it significant that he makes this remark to George in particular?

When Slim, Whit, Carlson and Curley come back to the bunk-house there's a lot of bad feeling in the air. Curley starts half-apologizing to Slim for his suspicions; but, when he's taunted by Carlson and Candy, he gets ready to lose his temper again. Why does he pick on Lennie in the end? And how does Lennie react? Do you remember why Lennie reacts in this way? (If not, look back to p. 29.)

Re-read the description of the fight on pp. 63 and 64, making notes on what happens. Then write an account of the fight from Lennie's point of view. Remember to include all the main things that happened and how you, as Lennie, felt at these different points.

Once the fight is over, Lennie backs against the wall. He has won the fight; but does he feel triumphant and pleased with himself? Have you ever felt similar things to Lennie after you've won a fight?

Slim makes arrangements for Curley to be taken to a doctor; but, before he is taken away, Slim makes Curley promise not to tell his father that it was Lennie who hurt his hand. How does Slim manage to get Curley to promise this?

Did you notice that George says something particularly important when he's explaining why Lennie did so much damage to Curley's hand? Slim (p. 65) has assumed that Lennie was very angry; but George says, no, it wasn't anger Lennie felt – it was fear. Remember that much the same thing happened in the struggle with the girl in Weed? Lennie, it seems, is at his most dangerous when he's afraid.

Do you believe Lennie when he says that he "didn't mean no harm"? Why have you made this decision? What is Lennie most afraid of happening as a result of the fight?

Scene 4: *pp. 66–83*

Crooks, the ranch hand based in the barn (the "stable buck"), lives in a little one-room lean-to beside the barn itself. The description of his room (pp. 66–7) tells us quite a lot about his interests and how he spends his time. Note down a list of some of the objects in the room, along with ideas on what these objects tell us about Crooks.

Crooks is at home, alone, on Saturday evening, rubbing ointment into his twisted back. (Do you remember how he damaged his back? If not, look back to p. 20.) When Lennie appears in the doorway, Crooks angrily tells him to go away. What are the reasons Crooks gives Lennie for this unfriendly reception? Do you think that if you were in Crooks's place, you would react in the same way?

Lennie tells him that the other ranch hands, including George, have gone into town for the evening. What reasons does Lennie give for coming to the barn? Is Crooks satisfied with these reasons? Why does Crooks ask Lennie into his room in the end?

From the start of the conversation, Crooks makes it clear that he doesn't believe in any of Lennie's schemes or plans. He seems much more interested in finding out more about the friendship that exists between Lennie and George. Do you get the feeling at this point (p. 70) that Crooks is behaving a bit like an interrogator who asks questions not out of friendly interest but for some other, perhaps sinister, purpose?

As he talks on, we begin to get some idea of what this purpose might be. Crooks, it appears, has always led a pretty isolated life: in his youth he was the only black child among many white children and now, as an adult, he is the only black hand on the ranch. During his life he has learned to mistrust white people (see the sentence on p. 70, "But I know now") and therefore avoid them as much as possible. But he has not been able to escape the miseries of loneliness. And so, when he sees a close friendship between two other people, he is overcome with envy and finds the sight of such friendship difficult to bear.

Would you agree that it's probably for this reason that Crooks torments Lennie with suggestions that he may be abandoned by George? How does Lennie react to Crooks's "supposin'" about George? Why does he react in this way, do you think?

Once Lennie is no longer threatening violence, Crooks goes on to explain that he only wanted Lennie to get an idea of the loneliness felt by him, Crooks. Crooks then describes just how he feels during his long evenings alone. Have you ever experienced anything like the feelings he describes? If you're black, describe any occasion when you too felt excluded from some activity or group "'cause you was black" (p. 72). If you're white, describe any occasion when it occurred to you to wonder if someone was being excluded from an activity or group because of the colour of their skin.

Lennie is barely half-listening to what Crooks is saying; but as soon as Crooks starts describing his peaceful childhood home, Lennie's interest is attracted. Would you agree that both have dream ranches in their minds – but Crooks's dream is in the past and Lennie's is in the future? Crooks goes on to explain why he is so impatient with Lennie's plans for the future. What are the reasons he gives?

When Candy appears, looking for Lennie, Crooks greets him in an abrupt and unfriendly way, just as he at first greeted Lennie. We learn, however, that really Crooks is delighted to have visitors. It turns out that, although Candy and Crooks have worked on the same ranch for years, this is the first time that Candy has been in Crooks's room. How does Candy react to the invitation to come into the room? ("I do' know" means 'I don't know': the apostrophe shows that a letter has been dropped.) And how does Crooks respond to Candy's embarrassment? (Explain the humour in Crooks's remark beginning, "Sure, . . . and a manure pile . . .")

Crooks resumes his attack on their plans. What sort of thing does he say to try to discourage Lennie and Candy? Why do you think he is attacking them in this way? Does he succeed in discouraging them? Read Candy's speech on p. 76 and make notes on why Candy is so determined that their dreams will come true.

Crooks is clearly taken aback to hear that nearly all the money needed to buy the place is already saved. Always in the past, it seems, men who seem to be desperate for their own land have in fact wasted their money in brothels and gambling dens. What offer does Crooks go on to make to Lennie and Candy?

When Curley's wife appears, it soon becomes clear that she's not really looking for her husband; she knows very well that Curley has gone to town with the rest of the men. How does she explain the fact that the ranch hands – apart from Lennie – don't like to be seen talking to her? Look on p. 78 at what Curley's wife has to say about her life; then, imagining that you're her, write notes, then a paragraph, about what it's like being married to Curley. Do you feel sorry for her or not? Why do you feel this way?

Curley's wife doesn't hesitate to insult the three men in front of her. How do the men react to these insults? Make sure that you describe the differences in their reactions. What gives Candy the courage to talk back to the boss's daughter-in-law? Do you think he's ever done such a thing before? Although Curley's wife scornfully rejects what he has to say, you may feel that at the end of the conversation it is Candy who emerges with dignity. Why might you feel this?

Curley's wife has already made it clear that she doesn't believe the story that Curley's hand was caught in a machine. Seeing the bruises on Lennie's face she now guesses correctly that he was the "machine" in question. Is she angry with Lennie for hurting her husband? If not, how does she seem to feel towards him?

When Crooks too finds the courage to ask her to leave them alone, Curley's wife turns on him with a viciousness we haven't seen before. Did you catch what she meant when she asked, "You know what I could do?" She meant that simply by claiming that Crooks, a black man, had tried to assault her, she could send him to a hideous death by lynching (that is, illegal hanging). Such murders by white lynch mobs were by no means uncommon in the USA at that time.

How do Crooks, Candy and Lennie react to this threat? After Curley's wife has gone, the atmosphere has changed in Crooks's room. How would you describe the change? How do you account for it? Are you surprised when, after George has collected Lennie and Candy, Crooks calls out to Candy to forget about his previous offer to work with them on the ranch? Why does he do this?

Scene 5: *pp. 84–98*

When we first enter the barn on Sunday afternoon, it seems a very pleasant place to be. It's full of hay, the horses are making contented noises; from outside we can hear the sounds of men happily playing horseshoes. But then we see something that gives us a shock. What do we see?

Lennie is clearly upset that the puppy is dead. But he feels a number of other emotions as well. Here's a list of some of the things he feels; put them in the order in which he expresses them.

1. A faint hope that George won't be angry with him.
2. Regret and sorrow that he hadn't paid more attention to the advice given him about the puppy by George and Slim.
3. Fear that, if he finds out what has happened, George won't let him look after the rabbits.
4. Realization that George will know that he, Lennie, is responsible for the puppy's death.
5. Grief over his growing conviction that the death of the puppy means that he'll never be allowed to look after the rabbits.
6. Anger with the puppy for letting itself be killed.
7. Belief that he can pretend to George that he, Lennie, had nothing to do with the puppy's death.

Unnoticed by Lennie, Curley's wife comes into the barn. How does Lennie react when he first sees her? Although she seems keen to talk to him, he is determined not to be drawn into conversation with her. What reasons does he give for this? How does she try to persuade him that it's all right for him to talk to her? (A "tenement" is a 'tournament', a series of games at the end of which a winner is declared.)

Curley's wife is rather taken aback when she discovers what Lennie is hiding. Write a paragraph explaining how the puppy died. How does she try to cheer up Lennie?

When Lennie is still unwilling to talk to her, Curley's wife gets angry. Re-read, on pp. 88–9, what she says about herself and her life. First make notes on what we learn about her earlier life; then write a paragraph describing the main events. Do you believe that the man in "pitchers" ('pictures', 'films') really did think she was a "natural" as an actress? Why else might he have said this? Do you think that her mother (her "ol' lady") really did steal the letter? If not, what do you think happened?

Do you feel any differently towards Curley's wife now that you know more about her? What words would you use to describe her? Does her eagerness to speak about herself without interruption remind you of anyone else in the story – of Crooks, for example, in the previous scene?

Lennie has claimed that he is listening to her; do you think that he really is? What do you think is actually going on in Lennie's mind? When the conversation turns from rabbits to the other kinds of things Lennie likes to pet, you may feel that danger is brewing. In his excitement, Lennie has clearly quite forgotten George's strict instructions not to talk to Curley's wife. How does Curley's wife react to Lennie's dropping his guard against her? What do you think she wants from Lennie?

Re-read the account of what happens from when Lennie first strokes the woman's hair up to the time when he realizes that she is dead (that is, the bottom of p. 91). First make notes on the different things that happen; then write a paragraph describing exactly what happens.

How did you feel when you read the account first of all? Although shocking, the sequence of events may have seemed quite familiar to you. You were remembering, perhaps, what we were told earlier about several other events: the 'attack' on the girl in Weed, for example; the death of Lennie's pet mice when he was a boy; the wounding of Curley; and, most recently, the death of the puppy. Note down the most important things that all these events have in common.

What are Lennie's reactions once he realizes that Curley's wife is dead? Are these the reactions that you would expect from him? Why?

After Lennie has gone to hide in the brush, the barn becomes peaceful once again. Even Curley's wife is peaceful in death. What is the first thing that old Candy thinks when he comes into the barn and sees Curley's wife?

George too thinks at first that Curley's wife is asleep; but, as soon as he realizes that she is dead, he also realizes how she met her death. Why do you think George says, on p. 94, "I should of knew . . ."? What does George think should be done about Lennie? Why does he think this?

And how does Candy respond to this suggestion? How do you think George feels when Candy mentions the likelihood of a lynching?

The worst moment for Candy comes when George confirms by his silence that the dream ranch will now never be bought. Candy is haunted by the thought of the happy life that will now never happen; George, on the other hand, has his eyes only too clearly fixed on the reality of the life that awaits him. What kind of life is that likely to be?

George says that "Lennie never done it in meanness . . ." What do you think he means by the word "meanness"? Do you agree with this judgement of Lennie?

After George and Candy have made arrangements to 'cover' George from suspicion of being involved in the killing, Candy pours out his anger and sorrow in a speech to the dead woman. Write a paragraph describing the different emotions he expresses. Do you think that he's fair to the dead woman? If she were alive, how do you think that she might answer old Candy?

Candy then leaves to fetch the other ranch hands. Re-read the description (p. 96) of Curley's first reaction to the sight of his wife's dead body. How would you describe this reaction? Is it the reaction you would expect from a husband who really cared for his wife?

George and Slim discuss the different options open to them for dealing with the problem of Lennie. Note down the different alternatives, along with the arguments for and against them.

When Carlson appears, shouting that Lennie has stolen his Luger pistol, you may suspect that he has picked on the wrong man. Who do you think has taken the gun? Why do you think this?

The search party sets out, armed with a shotgun at least, leaving Candy behind with the dead body. Why do you think "Curley's face reddened" (p. 98) when he refused to stay with the body? Watching the face of the dead woman, Candy murmurs "poor bastard". Who is he thinking of, do you think, as he utters these words? Why do you think this?

Scene 6: *pp. 99–107*

As the end of the story approaches, you'll see that we've come full circle as far as the setting is concerned. Back at the deep green pool by the Salinas river, we are once again looking at how nature occupies itself when there are no human beings present.

When Lennie appears, he comes "as silently as a creeping bear moves"; and the impression we have of him drinking from the pool is almost that of a weary animal. Do you think this is a suitable image for Lennie? Why?

Lennie is talking to himself – perhaps to reassure himself and to make himself feel less alone and frightened. He expresses several different feelings about his situation; note down the different feelings as he expresses them.

After this, rather an extraordinary thing happens. Lennie's imagination gives birth to a human figure, a little old woman, who proceeds to scold him. And this figure, we soon find out, is Lennie's Aunt Clara (we already know that she is now dead but that she looked after Lennie when he was young).

Why might Lennie be visited by a vision of Aunt Clara at this particular time? Would you agree that it might be partly because he's alone (we've already seen that Lennie doesn't like being alone; remember his evening visit to Crooks?) and partly because he feels that he has let George down particularly badly?

Write an account of the conversation between Lennie and the imaginary Aunt Clara. When you've done this, give a few moments' thought to two things. One is that it's most unlikely that the real Aunt Clara would use such powerful swear words! Such details make it clear to us that Lennie has indeed 'made her up' and is actually scolding himself. The other point is to do with what "Aunt Clara" says in the paragraph (p. 101) beginning, "All the time he coulda . . ." Look back to the top of p. 95 where George gives his own description of how his life will be without Lennie; how do these two accounts compare? Would you agree that it's clear that, although George used to be fond of telling Lennie how pleasant his life would be without him, he didn't really mean it at all?

The appearance of the imaginary giant rabbit marks the rise of further strong feelings of guilt and fear within Lennie. Note down the fears that the rabbit forces Lennie to confront.

George then comes out of the undergrowth and calms Lennie down. The first few moments of their conversation are rather different from usual – and clearly very different to what Lennie is expecting. What differences would you pick out as important? Have you included the fact that this time it is George rather than Lennie who is distracted and doesn't have much to say? As you read this section, did you pick up the reference to the "sound of men shouting to one another"? Who are these shouts coming from and what is the significance of them?

Lennie is relieved that George isn't going to leave him, but he's clearly puzzled that George doesn't seem to want to "give him hell". Why is it, do you think, that George has no inclination to get angry with Lennie? In the end, George is persuaded to say the things he usually says when he's in a rage with Lennie; but he speaks with difficulty and without feeling. Note down some examples of this.

Lennie then persuades George to speak about his favourite subject: the way in which he and George are different from the other ranch hands. (Remember when this was first mentioned, with the two of them sitting in the same place as they are now? Look back to p. 14 if you've forgotten that conversation.) Again, George is having difficulty in getting his words out. Why is this? How does George's shaky way of speaking make you feel?

What prompts George to tell Lennie to take off his hat? What is in George's mind, do you think? We now learn for sure that it was George – not Lennie – who took Carlson's Luger. As Lennie looks towards the mountains, George is intending to shoot him in the back of the head. Why has George decided to do this? Do you remember what old Candy said to George (p. 61) about wishing that he had shot his dog himself? How do you think this may have affected George? Do you think that George has made the right decision? Why?

For the last time, George and Lennie tell each other the story of their dream ranch. Can you explain why many people find this passage very moving? Look at the dialogue from the top of p. 105 down to the point where George finishes speaking. You'll see that there's a double meaning in nearly everything that George says. George seems to be talking about the same things as Lennie, but he's also preparing himself for something that Lennie doesn't know is about to happen: that is, Lennie's own death. Make notes on the double meanings involved.

Like Candy's old dog, Lennie doesn't "feel a thing" when he is shot. But George clearly does. What mixture of emotions do you imagine George feels? How would you feel in his place?

Slim is the only one of the ranch hands to show any sign of understanding what George must be going through. How does he try to comfort him? The last word is left to Carlson, the man who insisted earlier on shooting Candy's dog. Why do you think that this rather insensitive character is allowed to end the story in the way he does?

Characters

George

Because George, like Lennie, is one of the two central characters, it's not possible to get a full view of what kind of person he is just by reading a few selected sections of the book. We can get to know George only by paying careful attention throughout the story both to how we see him behave and to what is said about him, by himself and others.

The first time we meet George is on the Thursday evening in the clearing by the deep green pool. He's trying to persuade Lennie not to drink too much water: he knows that the water may not be fresh, but Lennie clearly doesn't understand that it may make him sick. You may well feel that this episode tells us a great deal about the kind of person George is, especially when he is with Lennie. Perhaps you would find it helpful to start off by writing down some words to describe how George comes across to us in this early part of the story. Would you agree that the words 'sensible', 'anxious', 'protective' and 'patient' are appropriate ones here? Now add your own suggestions to the list. Do you think that you could cope with Lennie as well as George seems to here?

Do you remember what Slim says about the friendship between George and Lennie? "It jus' seems kinda funny a cuckoo like him and a smart little guy like you travelin' together" (p. 39). It's certainly true, isn't it, that George does seem to be "a smart little guy"? After all, it's George who got them the jobs at the ranch; it's George who coped with the ugly situation in Weed when the girl was almost badly hurt by Lennie; it's George who can deal with bosses and difficult workmates.

If you re-read the section on pp. 40–42, you'll see that Slim was indeed right to call George "a smart little guy". However, you'll probably also find another way of seeing George reflected in these pages; you may recognize a feeling that we've come across before in the story and a feeling that will be expressed very powerfully during later events. How would you describe this feeling? Would you agree that it's something like *need* on George's part? Although George likes to pretend sometimes that Lennie is nothing but a nuisance to him (see p. 11, for example), the truth is that he needs Lennie just as much as Lennie needs him. In what ways do you think George does need Lennie? Give some examples from different parts of the story. One example might be that through the continuing story of the dream ranch, George and Lennie help each other to escape from the harsh reality of the life led by most ranch hands. What are the aspects of this life that George is most eager to escape?

Think about George's decision at the end of the book to shoot Lennie. What feelings do you think lay behind this decision? Write a paragraph to explain how shooting his friend could possibly be understood as a final proof of friendship on George's part.

Imagine that you can go forward in time ten years from the end of the story. Write a paragraph on how you think George is living then. Has he settled down in a place of his own, or is he still moving from ranch to ranch? Is he lonely or does he have at least one good friend? Does he still have dreams about the future?

Lennie

Think about some of the destructive things that we see Lennie doing – or hear about him doing – during the course of the story. He used to crush pet mice to death, for example; when in Weed he hurt – or at least badly frightened – a young woman; he kills his puppy by accident; and, in the end, he breaks a young woman's neck. How does knowing about these things make you feel about Lennie? Do you think of him as a frightening, cruel person? If not, how would you explain why you *don't* feel these things?

Perhaps your answer to that question echoes what George says about

Lennie on p. 95: "All the time he done bad things but he never done one of 'em mean." Lennie never *intends* to hurt anyone or anything; his problem is that he easily gets into a panic and when he's in this state he completely forgets that his great strength makes him very dangerous. Do you remember something else that George says about Lennie? On p. 43 he says, "There ain't no more harm in him than a kid . . . , except he's so strong." Note down some of the ways in which you think Lennie thinks and behaves like a child.

Did you include the fact that Lennie is very open and friendly to the people he meets? Like a child, he expects people to like him and to be nice to him. Think, for example, of his Saturday evening visit to Crooks when he is puzzled and dismayed by Crooks's unfriendly reception. What effect does this friendly approach have on other people? Would you agree that most people (including Crooks in the end) respond warmly to Lennie's affectionate nature and in turn show the best sides of their own natures? Try to think of some examples of this happening.

One obvious example can be found in the passage on p. 40, where George describes to Slim how Lennie jumped into the Sacramento River just because George told him to; and how Lennie's lack of resentment towards George made George ashamed of the way he had treated Lennie. It's clear that Lennie is almost totally dependent on George just as he was on his Aunt Clara. If George were not there to look after him, then Lennie would indeed probably end up in a "booby hatch", as Crooks suggests (p. 72). Would you agree that nowadays Lennie would be regarded as being 'mentally retarded'? Do you know any people who could be described in this way? How do you think about them and feel towards them? Does getting to know the character of Lennie make any difference to your attitudes?

Curley

We learn about Curley at six main points in the book: pp. 25–8, 37, 53–4, 61–5, 78 and 96–8. Look through these sections again carefully before you read on.

You'll probably have noticed that our first impressions of Curley are very much coloured both by George's reactions to him and by what Candy has to say about him. Do you think that George and Candy are good judges of character? Do you feel inclined to trust their judgement of Curley? Note down the main things that we learn about Curley from George and Candy.

You probably feel that George and Candy are proved right by later events. Curley does indeed continue to behave like a man who has a grudge against the world; he quite unfairly picks on Lennie for a fight, thinking that Lennie is too timid a character to fight back; and his lack of grief at his wife's death shows clearly that he saw her as a prize to fight over rather than a human being to love.

Can you imagine what it feels like to be Curley? Why do you think that he might behave in the way he does? Does Curley remind you of anyone you know? How do you feel about this person?

Curley's Wife

We learn about Curley's wife at five main points in the book: pp. 27–8, 31–2, 51, 77–82, 86–91. Look through these sections again carefully before you read on.

As with the character of Curley, you'll have noticed that the information we're given about Curley's wife is heavily coloured by the views of the different men who describe her. What is the view taken of her by the three characters who have most to say about her – Candy, Whit and George? Why is it, do you think, that these three men hold very similar views? Do you feel that, as seems to be the case with Curley, there really is little that can be said about her except that she's a trouble-maker? While thinking about that, remember that she is the only woman among several men, most of them unmarried; it may strike you that any woman, whatever her personality, might find it difficult to feel at ease in this situation. Remember too that George has a special reason (his knowledge of what happened in Weed) to be afraid of the presence of a woman in a place where Lennie lives and works.

Curley's wife, you'll have noticed, is not even given a name of her own; she is known to us only by association with a man whom she doesn't even like (p. 89). From what she tells Lennie about her life and from the way that we see her behave, would you describe her as a happy or an unhappy person? If you've decided that you would describe her as an unhappy person, go on to give some examples of how her unhappiness causes her to behave in ways that upset other people.

Do you know anyone who reminds you of Curley's wife in any way? Have you ever thought that this person might be unhappy?

Crooks

We learn about Crooks, the stable buck, at three main points of the book: pp. 19–20, 50 and 66–83. Look through these sections again carefully before you read on.

You'll probably agree that the first things we're told about Crooks are very important for understanding his character. Do you remember the main things that Candy tells George about Crooks? He says that because Crooks is black, he gets the brunt of the boss's bad temper; he also tells George that Crooks suffers from a twisted back as a result of being kicked by a horse. If these were the only facts that you knew about Crooks, what kind of person might you expect him to be? Might you expect him to be open and friendly, for example?

During the course of the Saturday evening in Crooks's room (pp. 66–83), we discover a great deal about the stable buck's life, past and present. We soon learn, for example, that he is far from being open and friendly in his approach to people; but we also learn that, like Curley's wife, he is an unhappy and lonely person. Give some examples of how Crooks's unhappiness and loneliness cause him to behave in ways that upset other people.

Just as Curley's wife is the only woman on the ranch, so Crooks is the only black person; both suffer from a sense of isolation from other people. However, where Curley's wife has power – being white and also the daughter-in-law of the boss – Crooks can do very little to gain people's respect. Think for a moment about what happens when Crooks does stand up for himself and his new friends (p. 80). Imagining that you are Crooks, write a paragraph explaining how you feel after Curley's wife has made her terrible threat.

Candy

We learn about Candy at six main points in the book: pp. 18–21, 24–8, 43–9, 58–62, 74–83 and 93–8. Look through these sections again carefully before you read on.

Like Crooks, Candy suffers from an injury at work: he lost his right hand in an accident. This means that, being crippled as well as old, he expects the boss to get rid of him quite soon. If this happens, he will have no home and only a little money saved up. How do you think John Steinbeck would like us to feel about this situation? Why do you think this?

Candy clearly keeps his eyes and ears open about the ranch: he knows a lot about what's going on, and he's quite willing to talk about what he knows to someone, like George, whom he considers to be a safe listener. However, Candy is usually careful to keep a low profile, avoiding any trouble or rows. Why is this, do you think? Would you agree that it's because, like Crooks, Candy feels that he is always in a weak position? Give some examples of occasions when Candy tries to remain unnoticed or otherwise shows that he feels powerless.

One of your examples may have involved Candy's attempt to shield his dog from Carlson's attention; and, on his failure to do this, his silent retreat to his bunk. What does Candy's dog mean to him, do you think? You'll probably agree that the dog is his best and oldest friend. Have you also considered the fact that Candy sees the way his dog is treated as a sign of the way he himself is regarded by others – for example, as old, worn-out, worthless?

Candy responds immediately and passionately to the dream which is so important to Lennie and George. Note down the different reasons why you think the dream ranch gripped his imagination so powerfully. What do you think will happen to Candy after his hopes are so cruelly dashed?

Themes

Friendship versus Loneliness

Think for a moment about the main characters in *Of Mice and Men*: George, Lennie, Candy, Crooks, Curley and Curley's wife. Which characters would you describe as lonely people? After answering that question, you may be surprised at the number of characters whom you do think of as lonely; and you'll probably have noticed that even if some of the characters are not lonely while the action of the story takes place, they were either very lonely in the past or they will be lonely in the future.

Would you agree that part of the message of the story is that people can still feel lonely even if they're surrounded by other people for much of the time? Think of Curley's wife, for example; although she has a husband, she can still say, "Think I don't like to talk to somebody ever' once in a while?" (p. 77). Or think of Candy, an old man who lives with other people but whose best friend is a dog. Have you ever felt lonely even though you were surrounded by people – at school, for example, or at a party? Write a paragraph describing the occasion and how you felt.

Let's turn now to thinking about how loneliness can affect people. We hear about this a great deal during the story – and we see some of the effects of loneliness actually taking place. Do you remember what George says about ranch hands? Re-read the passage on p. 13 that starts, "Guys like us, that work on ranches, are the loneliest guys in the world . . ." Re-read too the passage at the top of p. 41, starting with the words, "I ain't got no people . . ." George is giving his opinion here that lonely men easily become aggressive and difficult characters. Can you think of examples of this happening in the book?

Crooks too describes vividly the effects of loneliness: "I tell ya," he cried, "I tell ya a guy gets too lonely an' he gets sick" (p. 73). Re-read what Crooks has to say about loneliness on pp. 72 and 73. Would you agree that part of what he's describing is how loneliness has indeed made him "sick"? Do you think that Curley's wife could also be described as "sick" from the same cause? Write a paragraph explaining what you would mean by this. In real life, have you ever met people whom you think might be "sick" from loneliness?

Something else that the book tells us about loneliness is how people can be so desperate for a listener that they hardly notice whether or not the other person is really interested in what they have to say. Can you think of any examples of this happening in the story? Several one-sided conversations may have come to your mind in thinking about this. There is that last, fateful, conversation between Lennie and Curley's wife, for example (pp. 86–91), where both people are too preoccupied with their own thoughts and worries to pay much attention to what the other person is trying to communicate. Or there is the earlier conversation between Lennie and Crooks (pp. 68–74) where Crooks not only takes advantage of Lennie's presence to talk about his life but also acknowledges exactly what it is that he is doing. Do you remember what Crooks says about this? "I seen it over an' over an' over – a guy talkin' to another guy and it don't make no difference if he don't hear or understand. The thing is, they're talkin', or they're settin' still not talkin'. It don't make no difference, no difference" (p. 71).

What do you feel about what Crooks says here? Have you ever felt glad of another person's presence even if you knew they didn't really understand your state of mind at the time?

Having looked at some of the effects of loneliness on people, let's think now about what the book tells us about the difference friendship and kindness can make to people's lives. Take Candy and Crooks, for example. Think for a moment about what sort of people they seemed to be when we first got to know them; then write a paragraph describing how they changed when they felt that other people had begun to take an interest in them.

You'll probably have noted down something like that both men showed a renewed interest in life and a new self-confidence. Where previously they had been locked up inside themselves with their worries and suspicions, once they were shown friendship they began to open out to the opportunities that the world might still offer them.

The most important friendship in the book, of course, is that between Lennie and George. In different ways, each helped the other to cope with life. Would you agree that John Steinbeck's account of this friendship, along with the others described in the book, conveys a message that nearly all human beings have a deep need for affection and respect? Do you agree with this view?

Dreams versus Reality

Day-dreaming is important to most of the characters in *Of Mice and Men*. Lennie and George share a day-dream – about a small ranch that they will own one day – and the sharing makes the dream particularly powerful. As they discuss how they will live in the future, they encourage each other to heap up the detail, the place of their dreams all the time becoming more and more vivid in their minds.

Other characters have no one willing to share their dreams – but they continue to dream all the same. Think of Curley's wife, for example: she's constantly looking for opportunities to show the people around her that she's ill-suited to the restricted and boring life that she leads. In her head, she's a gifted actress who could have had a fabulously successful career in films. Or think of Crooks: his dreams focus on the past rather than the future, a past where he was surrounded by friends and relations and didn't know the meaning of loneliness. Even Curley – whom you may feel is the book's most unattractive character – can be seen to have his dream: that of being the 'hard man' of the ranch, feared and respected by everyone.

The dream cherished by George and Lennie is one, we learn, shared by a good many ranch hands. Do you remember what Crooks says about this? He tells Lennie: "I seen hunderds of men come by on the road an' on the ranches with their bindles on their back an' that same damn thing in their heads. Hunderds of them. They come, an' they quit an' go on; an' every damn one of 'em's got a little piece of land in his head" (p. 74). What is it about this particular dream, do you think, that is so attractive to these men? After answering this question, take a minute to think about your own friends or fellow students. Is there a dream that you all have in common? What is this dream and why is it so important to you all?

In *Of Mice and Men*, the day-dreams remain just that – day-dreams: none of them are transformed into reality. Just like all the other ranch hands, George, Lennie and Candy are doomed never to set foot on their own piece of land. Curley's wife will never be an actress. Curley will continue to attract scorn rather than respect. And Crooks is almost certain to end his days a lonely man. Whenever dreams are put to the test in this book, they evaporate, disappear. Think, for example, of the scene in Crooks's room where Curley's wife viciously crushes the growing confidence of Crooks and Candy; or think how George and Lennie's dream begins to approach reality – only to be destroyed entirely.

Despite this, however, you may feel that the author is not suggesting that it's a waste of time to dream. Note down some of the positive aspects of day-dreaming shown in the story. You may want to include, for example, the fact that day-dreaming prevents some of the characters from falling into despair. Do any of the positive aspects you have noted down apply to day-dreaming in your own life? In what way?

Injustice

In discussing the theme of 'injustice', we come to some of the reasons why the characters in *Of Mice and Men* find day-dreams so important in their lives.

Think of everything we're told about the lives of the ranch hands, for example. They are rootless men without a permanent home; they move from ranch to ranch, living with strangers on other people's property – and even eating food cooked always by other people. There's much hard work but little pleasure in their lives – so, when they save up a little money, the great temptation is always to spend it quickly in bar rooms and brothels. It's hardly surprising then that many of them dream of owning a little piece of land of their own.

Do you remember what Candy says about his working life? "I planted crops for damn near ever'body in this state, but they wasn't my crops, and when I harvested 'em, it wasn't none of my harvest" (p. 76). And do you remember too the situation Candy is in as he approaches an old age when he can no longer work? He has lost a hand in an accident at work and has been given a little compensation; but he knows that he'll soon be forced to leave the ranch and, as he says, "I won't have no place to go, an' I can't get no more jobs."

What do you think is the message that John Steinbeck is trying to convey through his descriptions of Candy and the other ranch hands? Would you agree that one of the things he is suggesting is that people who work hard and long deserve better than a life spent entirely at other people's service and an old age of poverty and despair? What are your own views on this subject? Why do you feel this way?

Let's look at another example of injustice to be found in the story. Crooks is black – and is clearly discriminated against because of his colour.

The boss takes out his rages on him; the other ranch hands pick on him, excluding him from card games in the bunk-house, for example. Curley's wife makes a dreadful threat against him: she threatens to accuse him of assaulting her and thus ensure that he will be lynched. Crooks knows well that the fact that the accusation is completely false would in no way save him from this dreadful fate. Black men and their families at that time had no reason to expect justice from their white compatriots; such threats therefore were a recurring nightmare for them.

Do you think that John Steinbeck thinks it right that black people should be discriminated against because of their colour? You'll probably agree that the way in which the character of Crooks is presented suggests strongly that the author believes that racial discrimination is harmful to both the white and the black people involved. Do you think that, even if discrimination of this kind did occur in the past, it no longer does so today – or, certainly, not in Great Britain? Write a paragraph explaining why you hold the view you do.

Glossary

alfalfa: a kind of plant on which animals graze, similar to clover
ast: ask
averted: turned away
bindle: a blanket rolled up so that it can be carried easily across one's back, often with clothes and other possessons rolled up inside it; the word can also be used to refer to any package or bundle
bindle stiff: a hobo or tramp
blackjack: a card game
blowin' in our jack: losing our money
booby hatch: lunatic asylum
brighter 'n a bitch: very bright indeed
brush: undergrowth, brushwood
buck (barley, grain-bags, etc.): to carry or to throw
bullwhip: a long, plaited rawhide whip with a knotted end
bunk-house: sleeping quarters for ranch hands
burlap: a coarsely woven cloth made of fibres of jute, flax or hemp, and used to make sacks
can: to sack someone from a job
carp: a freshwater fish
cat-house: brothel
contorted: twisted
'coons: racoons, small wild animals related to the bear
'cots: apricots
derogatory: slighting, slightly scornful
disarming: charming
eatin' on: eating at, bothering
euchre: a card game
fawning: very anxious to please
fifty and found: fifty dollars a month pay, plus accommodation and food
figuring: doing sums, calculations with numbers
flats: stretches of sands sometimes submerged by water
floodwater wood: branches etc.

carried down by a river in flood
floosie: stupid, worthless
goo-goos: people whose skin colour is not white
grey-backs: lice
grizzled: grey
halter: a device that fits around the head or neck of an animal and can be used to lead or secure it
hame: one of the two curved wooden or metal pieces of the harness that fit round the neck of an animal pulling a load, and to which the trace chains are attached
hoosegow: jail
horseshoe game: a game where the players throw horseshoes, with the aim of hitting or getting near a metal stake
jail bait: a woman with whom sexual involvement would lead to serious trouble. "Jailbait all set on the trigger" refers to a situation where there's clear opportunity for sexual involvement; and this involvement would almost certainly result in very bad trouble
jerkline skinner: a mule driver who uses long reins to control several animals
jungle-up: make a camp
kewpie doll lamp: a lamp that looks like a certain kind of doll – small, fat-cheeked and wide-eyed, with a curl of hair on top of the head
liniment: a thin ointment
morosely: gloomily
mottled: of blotched or smudgy appearance
nail-key: a small barrel for nails
pants rabbits: lice
pendular: a weight hung so that it can swing freely
poop: stamina, energy
poundin' their tail: working very hard
pulp magazine: cheap, popular magazine
punks: inexperienced young men
rabbit in: to run in
raptly: in an entranced way
rassel: heave
reprehensible: blameworthy
rigidly: stiffly
roaches: cockroaches
rummy: a card game
scourges: pests
skinner: a mule driver
slough: hit hard
solitare: the card game, patience, which is played by one person only
stable buck: ranch hand in charge

of the animals and their equipment

stake: a comparatively large sum of money; an amount of money saved, borrowed or loaned to be used to start a new business

sullenly: in an angry, sulky way

swamper: odd-job man

ticking: a strong, tightly woven fabric of cotton or linen used especially to make pillow and mattress coverings

trace chains: one of two side chains connecting a harnessed animal to the vehicle it is pulling

two bits: a quarter (of a dollar) – 25 cents

vials: small containers for liquids

welter: welter-weight; a boxer over 10 stone (and not over 10 stone 8 pounds) (amateur)

wheeler: a wheel horse, the horse that follows the leader and is harnessed nearest to the front wheels

writhed: twisted

yammered: whined

yella-jackets: small wasps

Passage for Comparison

In this extract from the poem 'The Ballad of Reading Gaol' (1898) by Oscar Wilde, we can sense the poet's strong feeling that human love all too often ends in disaster. Once you've read the piece, perhaps you'd like to take one of the situations he describes and write about it from the victim's point of view?

Yet each man kills the thing he loves,
By each let this be heard,
Some do it with a bitter look,
Some with a flattering word,
The coward does it with a kiss,
The brave man with a sword!

Some kill their love when they are young,
And some when they are old;
Some strangle with the hands of Lust,
Some with the hands of Gold:
The kindest use a knife, because
The dead so soon grow cold.

Some love too little, some too long,
Some sell, and others buy;
Some do the deed with many tears,
And some without a sigh:
For each man kills the thing he loves,
Yet each man does not die.

Discussion Topics and Examination Questions

Discussion Topics

Your understanding and appreciation of this story will be much increased if you discuss aspects of it with other people. Here are some topics you could consider:

1. What do you feel were Steinbeck's motives in writing this story? What was he trying to make us think about? Does it have any relevance for us today?
2. Was George right or wrong in taking a potentially dangerous person such as Lennie with him into work situations among persons who did not know him?
3. Discuss the social conditions under which the characters live and the effect these have on their lives.

The Examination

You may find that the set texts chosen by your teacher for the examination have been selected from a very wide list of suggestions in the examination syllabus. The questions in the examination paper will therefore be applicable to many different books. Here are some questions you could answer by making use of *Of Mice and Men*.

1. Characters in stories are often led on by dreams of a wonderful future. From a book of your choice, explain what these are for

one or more of the characters and discuss what has happened to these dreams by the end of the story.

2. Write about a novel in which loneliness is an important theme. Show its effect on one or more of the leading characters and the part it plays in the story.
3. Choose a book where close friendship is put to a severe test. Briefly outline the situation and then comment on how the friends emerge from this testing.

Examination Questions on *Of Mice and Men*

1. How far was Lennie the victim of other people's faults?
2. Describe the incident when Curley attacks Lennie in the bunk-house. Explain how and why it began and make clear the reactions of Lennie, George and Slim.
3. Discuss George's feelings for Lennie. What do you think George gained from this difficult friendship?

READ MORE IN PENGUIN

In every corner of the world, on every subject under the sun, Penguin represents quality and variety – the very best in publishing today.

For complete information about books available from Penguin – including Puffins, Penguin Classics and Arkana – and how to order them, write to us at the appropriate address below. Please note that for copyright reasons the selection of books varies from country to country.

In the United Kingdom: Please write to *Dept. EP, Penguin Books Ltd, Bath Road, Harmondsworth, West Drayton, Middlesex UB7 ODA*

In the United States: Please write to *Consumer Sales, Penguin Putnam Inc., P.O. Box 12289 Dept. B, Newark, New Jersey 07101-5289.* VISA and MasterCard holders call 1-800-788-6262 to order Penguin titles

In Canada: Please write to *Penguin Books Canada Ltd, 10 Alcorn Avenue, Suite 300, Toronto, Ontario M4V 3B2*

In Australia: Please write to *Penguin Books Australia Ltd, P.O. Box 257, Ringwood, Victoria 3134*

In New Zealand: Please write to *Penguin Books (NZ) Ltd, Private Bag 102902, North Shore Mail Centre, Auckland 10*

In India: Please write to *Penguin Books India Pvt Ltd, 11 Community Centre, Panchsheel Park, New Delhi 110017*

In the Netherlands: Please write to *Penguin Books Netherlands bv, Postbus 3507, NL-1001 AH Amsterdam*

In Germany: Please write to *Penguin Books Deutschland GmbH, Metzlerstrasse 26, 60594 Frankfurt am Main*

In Spain: Please write to *Penguin Books S. A., Bravo Murillo 19, 1º B, 28015 Madrid*

In Italy: Please write to *Penguin Italia s.r.l., Via Benedetto Croce 2, 20094 Corsico, Milano*

In France: Please write to *Penguin France, Le Carré Wilson, 62 rue Benjamin Baillaud, 31500 Toulouse*

In Japan: Please write to *Penguin Books Japan Ltd, Kaneko Building, 2-3-25 Koraku, Bunkyo-Ku, Tokyo 112*

In South Africa: Please write to *Penguin Books South Africa (Pty) Ltd, Private Bag X14, Parkview, 2122 Johannesburg*

READ MORE IN PENGUIN

A CHOICE OF TWENTIETH-CENTURY CLASSICS

Ulysses James Joyce

Ulysses is unquestionably one of the supreme masterpieces, in any artistic form, of the twentieth century. 'It is the book to which we are all indebted and from which none of us can escape' T. S. Eliot

The First Man Albert Camus

'It is the most brilliant semi-autobiographical account of an Algerian childhood amongst the grinding poverty and stoicism of poor French-Algerian colonials' J. G. Ballard. 'A kind of magical Rosetta stone to his entire career, illuminating both his life and his work with stunning candour and passion' *The New York Times*

Flying Home Ralph Ellison

Drawing on his early experience – his father's death when he was three, hoboeing his way on a freight train to follow his dream of becoming a musician – Ellison creates stories which, according to the *Washington Post*, 'approach the simple elegance of Chekhov.' 'A shining instalment' *The New York Times Book Review*

Cider with Rosie Laurie Lee

'Laurie Lee's account of childhood and youth in the Cotswolds remains as fresh and full of joy and gratitude for youth and its sensations as when it first appeared. It sings in the memory' *Sunday Times*. 'A work of art' Harold Nicolson

Kangaroo D. H. Lawrence

Escaping from the decay and torment of post-war Europe, Richard and Harriett Somers arrive in Australia to a new and freer life. Somers, a disillusioned writer, becomes involved with an extreme political group. At its head is the enigmatic Kangaroo.

READ MORE IN PENGUIN

A CHOICE OF TWENTIETH-CENTURY CLASSICS

Belle du Seigneur Albert Cohen

Belle du Seigneur is one of the greatest love stories in modern literature. It is also a hilarious mock-epic concerning the mental world of the cuckold. 'A *tour de force*, a comic masterpiece weighted with an understanding of human frailty ... It is, quite simply, a book that must be read' *Observer*

The Diary of a Young Girl Anne Frank

'Fifty years have passed since Anne Frank's diary was first published. Her story came to symbolize not only the travails of the Holocaust, but the struggle of the human spirit ... This edition is a worthy memorial' *The Times*. 'A witty, funny and tragic book ... stands on its own even without its context of horror' *Sunday Times*

Herzog Saul Bellow

'A feast of language, situations, characters, ironies, and a controlled moral intelligence ... Bellow's rapport with his central character seems to me novel writing in the grand style of a Tolstoy – subjective, complete, heroic' *Chicago Tribune*

The Go-Between L. P. Hartley

Discovering an old diary, Leo, now in his sixties, is drawn back to the hot summer of 1900 and his visit to Brandham Hall ... 'An intelligent, complex and beautifully-felt evocation of nascent boyhood sexuality that is also a searching exploration of the nature of memory and myth' Douglas Brooks-Davies

Orlando Virginia Woolf

Sliding in and out of three centuries, and slipping between genders, Orlando is the sparkling incarnation of the personality of Vita Sackville-West as Virginia Woolf saw it.

READ MORE IN PENGUIN

A CHOICE OF TWENTIETH-CENTURY CLASSICS

Collected Stories Vladimir Nabokov

Here, for the first time in paperback, the stories of one of the twentieth century's greatest prose stylists are collected in a single volume. 'To read him in full flight is to experience stimulation that is at once intellectual, imaginative and aesthetic, the nearest thing to pure sensual pleasure that prose can offer' Martin Amis

Cancer Ward Aleksandr Solzhenitsyn

Like his hero Oleg Kostoglotov, Aleksandr Solzhenitsyn spent many years in labour camps for mocking Stalin and was eventually transferred to a cancer ward. 'What he has done above all things is record the truth in such a manner as to render it indestructible, stamping it into the Western consciousness' *Observer*

Nineteen Eighty-Four George Orwell

'A volley against the authoritarian in every personality, a polemic against every orthodoxy, an anarchistic blast against every unquestioning conformist ... *Nineteen Eighty-Four* is a great novel, and it will endure because its message is a permanent one' Ben Pimlott

The Complete Saki Saki

Macabre, acid and very funny, Saki's work drives a knife into the upper crust of English Edwardian life. Here are the effete and dashing heroes, Reginald, Clovis and Comus Bassington, tea on the lawn, the smell of gunshot and the tinkle of the caviar fork, and here is the half-seen, half-felt menace of disturbing undercurrents ...

The Castle Franz Kafka

'In *The Castle* we encounter a proliferation of obstacles, endless conversations, perpetual possibilities which hook on to each other as if intent to go on until the end of time' Idris Parry. 'Kafka may be the most important writer of the twentieth century' J. G. Ballard